Witches' Holiday

Remembering David who had witches
in his closet, and to his and Andy and
Kathy's father, Martin
—A.L.

For little turkey theo lumps
—T.T.

ISBN 0-590-46891-X

Text copyright © 1971 by Alice Low.
Illustrations copyright © 1997 by Tricia Tusa.
All rights reserved. Published by Scholastic Inc.
CARTWHEEL BOOKS and the CARTWHEEL BOOKS logo
are trademarks and/or registered trademarks of Scholastic Inc.

10 9 8 7 6 5 4 3 2 1

Printed in the U.S.A.   24
First printing, September 1997

Witches' Holiday

by Alice Low
Illustrated by Tricia Tusa

SCHOLASTIC INC. Cartwheel BOOKS ®
New York Toronto London Auckland Sydney

Three witches hide inside my closet.
Every night they thump around,
Waiting there to rope me in
To their witch-ditch dungeon underground.

But they can't get out,
For every night
I shut the door,
I shut it tight.
Then they stamp their feet
In a rage and shout—
"Mean Boy! Mean Boy!
Let us out!"

But then one night —
On Halloween —
They got the chance
They'd waited for.
I came home late,
So tired out
That I forgot
To shut the door.

I woke up to
A whooshing zoom,
And out they flew
Into my room.
They circled wildly
Overhead …

Then *crash!* They landed
On my bed:
One fat, one small,
One tall and thin.
Now, I thought,
They'll rope me in.

They stretched and yawned, kicked up their heels,
Rubbed their necks, and blinked their eyes.
"Space at last!" the head witch said.
"Come on, let's get some exercise."

"Simon says
Do this! Do that!"
They hopped, they climbed,
They swung, they sat,
Jumped on my bed
Like acrobats,
And bounced
On the tips
Of their pointed hats,
Till the fat witch cried,
"My hat is flat!
Squashed my hat,
Enough of that!
Grab his toys,
It's time to play.
Let's have a witches' holiday.

"His toys belong
To us tonight,
And if they break
It serves him right."
"That's right,"
They yelled.
"That boy was mean!
Let's have some fun
This Halloween!"

They finger-painted on my ceiling,
Crayoned pictures on my wall
With every crayon in the box,
And pressed so hard,
They broke them all.
They roller-skated
Down the hall.
They played my games,
And kicked my ball,
Till the air went out
With a long low hiss,
And the fat witch cried,
"Enough of this!
I'm absolutely
Starved," she said.
"It's been three days
Since we were fed."

The others shouted,
"We want eats!
Let's raid his bag,
It's filled with treats!"

They dumped my candy on the floor,
And snatched and tore and ate it fast.
They chomped and bit and chewed it up.
They didn't try to make it last.

They chanted as
They ate their fill,
"We'll eat it all,
We will! We will!

"Turkish taffy,
Lollipops!
Red hot dollars,
Lemon drops!
Peppermint and
Wintergreen,
And every kind of
Jelly bean!
Strawberry, raspberry,
Cherry-berry, chew!
Pink-berry, ink-berry,
Blackberry, blue!

"Red and green
And orange, too!
Every bean
For me, not you!
Now bite those sticks,
And chew that gum!
Now all together,
Yum! Yum! Yum!"

They chewed until
Their teeth fell out.
"Enough!" I heard
The fat witch shout.
"We chewed that gum,
We bit those sticks.
We've had our treats,
It's time for tricks.

"Outdoors!" she shouted. "Everyone,
Untie that rope and let's begin.
We'll use that rope for tricks and fun."
Now I was *sure* they'd rope me in.

They pulled the clothesline
Off the trees,
And chanted words
That went like these —
"Jump rope, lasso,
Tug of war!
So many things
A rope is for.

A rope is to climb,
A rope is a swing.
A rope in a loop
Is a hoop or a ring.

"A rope is an excellent
Tennis net.
You can dance on a rope,
You can pirouette.

A rope is a slope,
It's a hill to ski down.
You down, me down,
One, two, three down.

A rope is a slide
For a witch to slide on,
And best of all,
It's a road to ride on."

They rode my bike
Those witches did.
One, two, three
In a pyramid.
They weighed so much
That the tire went flat,
And the fat witch cried,
"Enough of that!
I'm black-and-blue,
I've bumped my head.
What's more,
I'm absolutely dead!

"To bed!" she said. "Fly home to bed!"
"We can't," they cried. "Our brooms are gone.
They're in his room. We can't climb up."
"We can!" the head witch said. "Come on!

"We'll use that rope
Just one more time.
Throw it! Hook it!
Ready? Climb!"

"Oh, no you don't,"
I shouted. "No!"
And I cut the rope
And shouted, "Go!
Take your brooms,
Your shoes, your cat.
Now fly away.
Enough of that!

"Fly away,
You witches, fly!
Good-bye for good,
Good-bye, good-bye."

And they echoed back
From the midnight sky,
"Good-bye for good,
Good-bye, good-bye."